After
HAPPILY
—EVER—
AFTER

Jack and the Bean Snacks

After Happily Ever After was published in the United States
in 2009 and 2014 by Stone Arch Books, A Capstone Imprint
1710 Roe Crest Drive, North Mankato, Minnesota 56003
www.capstoneyoungreaders.om

First published by Orchard Books, a division of Hachette Children's Books
338 Euston Road, London NW1 3BH, United Kingdom

Library of Congress Cataloging-in-Publication Data is available
on the Library of Congress website.

ISBN: 978-1-4342-7964-4 (paperback)

Summary: Jack is ready for another adventure, but what could be as
exciting as tricking the giant and stealing the golden goose? A trip to the
local forest superstore gives him some food for thought. Find out if Jack
can gain his mother's trust with his new plan.

Designer: Russell Griesmer
Photo Credits: ShutterStock/Maaike Boot, 5, 6, 7, 52, 53

Printed in the United States of America.
121417   010984R

After HAPPILY -EVER- AFTER

Jack and the Bean Snacks

by TONY BRADMAN

illustrated by SARAH WARBURTON

STONE ARCH BOOKS®
a capstone imprint

TABLE OF CONTENTS

So Jack defeated the giant,
grabbed the golden goose,
and lived happily ever after
with his mother.
And then ...

CHAPTER ONE

"Come on, Jack," said Mom. "Up the stairs and into your pajamas, please. It's time for bed. And don't forget to brush your teeth."

"But it's only seven o'clock!" cried Jack. "And do you have to talk to me like that, Mom? I am not a little boy anymore."

"Well, you are to me," said Mom. "Now up those stairs."

"But I'm a hero, Mom," said Jack. "I climbed the beanstalk, outwitted the terrifying giant, and got my picture in all the newspapers, remember?"

"How could I forget?" Mom sighed. "It could have been a disaster! You never think things through, Jack. I sent you to sell poor old Daisy the cow because we had no money, and all you came home with was a few beans."

"Magic beans," said Jack. "And everything worked out okay, didn't it? I brought you back a bag of gold, and a hen that lays golden eggs."

"Ha! The gold lasted a week, and that hen only lays an egg when she feels like it, which is about once a month," Mom snorted.

"So we're not as rich as everyone in the forest seems to think," she went on. "I don't get time to sit around watching TV, anyway. Not like some people I could mention."

"You liked the Singing Harp, though, didn't you?" Jack asked.

"Oh, yes," said Mom. "Until I discovered it sings the same song over and over again!"

"Now if you're not upstairs by the time
I count to five," she said.

"I'm going," Jack grumbled.

Later, Mom came up to check that Jack had brushed his teeth and give him a bedtime kiss.

Jack lay in bed, unable to sleep, wondering what he could do to make Mom treat him differently.

He remembered what she'd said about not having time to sit around, and suddenly he felt guilty. Perhaps if he helped her more she would feel better.

CHAPTER TWO

When Jack came down to breakfast the next morning, he heard his mom muttering.

"There just aren't enough hours in the day," she said. "How can I go to the supermarket and get the laundry done?"

"Don't worry, Mom," said Jack. "I'll do the shopping for you."

"I don't think so," Mom said, shaking her head. "What's brought this on, anyway?"

"I'd just like to help you," said Jack,
giving her a big smile. "And couldn't
you tell me what to do? I mean, it can't
be that hard, can it?"

"All right, then," said Mom. "Here's the list and some money. It's more than you'll need, so I expect to see plenty of change. Come straight back from the supermarket and don't talk to strangers, okay?"

"No problem, Mom," said Jack. "You can trust me."

At the supermarket, Jack grabbed a
cart and quickly made his way to the
fruit and vegetable section.

Mr. and Mrs. Goldilocks were already there, glumly examining the fruit.

"I'm sick of eating the same things all the time," said Mr. Goldilocks. "They don't have much variety here, do they?"

Jack looked around. He had to agree. So he moved on to the next section without picking up anything, even though fruit and vegetables were the first items on Mom's list.

He scanned the rest of the list and
frowned.

None of it was very exciting. What Mom needed was a little treat to cheer her up. A couple of big tubs of double chocolate chip ice cream should do the trick.

Half an hour later, Jack's cart was
overflowing with treats of all kinds —
ice cream, candy bars, chips, cookies,
cupcakes, and bottles of soda.

Jack had spent all of the money, and
he hadn't bought anything that was on
Mom's list.

CHAPTER THREE

When he got home, Mom was very, very angry with him. "What have you done?" she moaned.

Jack's smile vanished. "We can't live on stuff like this! Besides, I'm trying to lose weight."

"I was only trying to cheer you up, Mom," Jack muttered.

"Well, you've done exactly the opposite," she said. "I'll have to do the shopping all over again tomorrow, and we really can't afford to waste money. So you can go straight to bed without any supper."

That evening, Jack lay in bed, unable
to sleep, wondering what he should
do. Everything seemed to come back
to money. Mom was always worrying
about not having enough.

Maybe he should go on another
exciting adventure. He could win
enough treasure to make them rich
for the rest of their lives.

CHAPTER FOUR

The next morning, Jack came downstairs, ate his breakfast, and acted normal. He was waiting for Mom to leave for the supermarket.

"Goodbye, Jack," said Mom. "Be a good boy while I'm out, okay?"

"What makes you think I'd be anything else?" said Jack, smiling.

Mom rolled her eyes. And as soon as she left, Jack grabbed the hen that laid the golden eggs and ran off. He searched high and low for someone who could sell him more magic beans.

At last, a man listened to him. The man asked about the hen, then smiled.

"Magic beans?" he said. "No problem, kid. I've got loads!"

So Jack traded the magic hen for 100
beans. He had them planted long before
Mom got home.

That evening, to Mom's surprise, Jack
sent himself to bed early. In the morning,
he dashed downstairs. Mom was looking
out of the window.

"There you go, Mom," said Jack, proudly.
"All of our problems are solved! Well, they
will be as soon as I've climbed a few of
those huge beanstalks, outwitted some
more giants, and won lots of treasure!"

"Huge beanstalks?" asked Mom, puzzled. "All I see is a garden full of ordinary bean plants. Where did they come from? And where's the hen?"

"Oh no! I don't believe it!" moaned Jack,
looking out the window. "I've been tricked!"

Of course, Mom was extra angry with him when he told her what he'd done. Now that the hen was gone, they had nothing at all to live on.

"Jack, I know you're trying to help, but when are you going to learn to think before you do anything?" Mom said at last.

And with that, Mom stormed up the stairs and went to lie down.

CHAPTER FIVE

Jack trudged into the garden. He was
desperate to make Mom change her
mind about him. If only he hadn't traded
the hen for these tiny bean plants, he
thought as he kicked one of them.

A shower of beans fell onto the ground. And suddenly Jack remembered what Mr. Goldilocks had said at the supermarket.

Not enough variety, huh? Well, maybe the supermarket would like to sell beans! He hadn't seen any of them at the store. Jack ran off to get a basket.

Jack did sell his beans to the Forest
Superstore. He was very tempted to
spend all the profits on a present for
Mom, but he didn't. He thought about
what she'd said, and he bought a lot
more beans instead.

Within a few years, Jack's 100 beanstalks had made him the richest farmer in the forest. He was brilliant at coming up with ideas for new products and outwitting the competition.

His picture was in the papers all the time. And he always thought before he did anything now. So Mom never, ever had to worry about money again.

She was very proud of him. "That's my
son!" she would say to all the neighbors,
and she let him stay up as late as he
wanted. Well, almost.

And so, amazingly enough, Jack and his Mom really did live happily ever after!

THE

ABOUT THE AUTHOR

Tony Bradman writes for children of all ages. He is particularly well known for his top-selling Dilly the Dinosaur series. His other titles include the Happily Ever After series, *The Orchard Book of Heroes and Villains*, and *The Orchard Book of Swords, Sorcerers,* and *Superheroes*. Tony lives in South East London.

ABOUT THE ILLUSTRATOR

Sarah Warburton is a rising star in children's books. She is the llustrator of the Rumblewick series, which has been very well received at an international level. The series spans across both picture books and fiction. She has also illustrated nonfiction titles and the Happily Ever After series. She lives in Bristol, England, with her young baby and husband.